The ABCs of

Thanks and Please

by Diane C. Ohanesian
Illustrated by Margaret Chamberlain

Scholastic Inc.
New York   Toronto   London   Auckland
Sydney   Mexico City   New Delhi   Hong Kong

To Paul, who deserves all of my thanks! — D. O.

For my lovely friend Penny, who is always polite and charming. — M. C.

ISBN 978-0-545-37962-5

Text copyright © 2011 by Diane C. Ohanesian
Illustrations copyright © 2011 by Margaret Chamberlain

12 11 10 9 8   14 15 16/0

Printed in the U.S.A.   40
First printing, October 2011

You're growing and you're learning
and you want to do what's right.
These ABCs will help you,
every morning, noon, and night!

is for Asking
in a way that starts with "please."

B is for Believing
that it's not okay to tease.

C is for Caring
    for your friends and family, too.

is for Discussing
things that hurt and bother you.

is for Exploring
ways to play and get along.

 is for Forgiving
when a friend does something wrong.

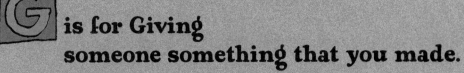

G is for Giving
someone something that you made.

H is for Hugging
when that someone feels afraid!

I is for Inviting
all your friends to have some fun.

J is for Joining.
See how fast the job gets done!

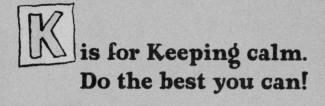

K is for Keeping calm.
Do the best you can!

L is for Listening
to someone else's plan.

M is for Meeting
and for greeting someone new.

is for Noticing
when someone's feeling blue.

 is for Obeying
rules that keep you safe each day.

P is for Protecting
a pal who's in the way!

Q is for Questioning
when you don't know why.

 is for Remembering.
You can do it if you try!

is for Sharing
a toy or favorite snack.

**is for Trying
not to take it back!**

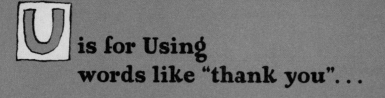

U is for Using
words like "thank you"...

. . . and "I'm sorry."

V is for Voting
when it's hard to choose a story.

W is for Waiting
when being first feels better.

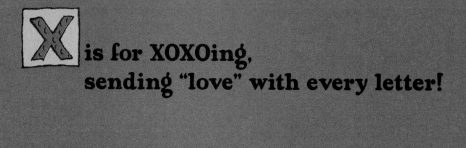

X is for XOXOing,
sending "love" with every letter!

Y is for Yelling
to your teammates, "You were great!"

Z is for Zipping
into bed without complaint!

You're growing and you're learning,
so each and every day
keep these ABCs in mind
and you'll be on your way!